Rhyme
Time

Queen
Rosie

First published in 2008 by
Franklin Watts
338 Euston Road
London
NW1 3BH

Franklin Watts Australia
Level 17/207 Kent Street
Sydney
NSW 2000

A CIP catalogue record for this book is available
from the British Library.

ISBN 978 0 7496 7943 9 (hbk)
ISBN 978 0 7496 7955 2 (pbk)

Series Editor: Jackie Hamley
Series Advisor: Dr Barrie Wade
Series Designer: Peter Scoulding

Printed in China

Franklin Watts is a division of
Hachette Children's Books,
an Hachette Livre UK company.

Queen Rosie

by Penny Dolan

Illustrated by Flory Denis

W
FRANKLIN WATTS
LONDON·SYDNEY

Queen Rosie loved pink.
She loved pink, pink, **pink!**

She lay in her bed,
and had a big think.

She had pinkest pink hair,

and pink clothes to wear.

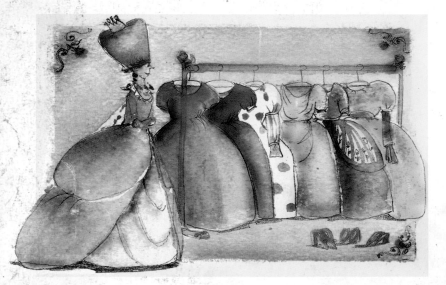

But she couldn't help wishing for pink everywhere!

So Queen Rosie jumped up
with a bellowing shout.

"My palace shall
be pink, both inside ...

11

"... and out!"

"Cooks, cook pink food!
I want everything pink!

"Pink food on my tables,
and pink drink to drink!"

"All must wear pink!"

So they did, young ...

... and old.

Any guest not in pink
was left out in the cold.

Though Queen Rosie
walked round with a
smile on her face,

not everyone liked pink
all over the place!

So the children went to see the wise man in the wood. "Could you help us please, Sir?"

He said that he could.

23

The Queen opened her gift.

"Surprise, surprise!"

She put those pink
spectacles over her eyes,

and was delighted to see
what she could see!

"At last my world's
perfect, as pink as can be!"

So everything went as the
wise man had planned,

and everyone else loved

their colourful land!

Leapfrog Rhyme Time has been specially designed to fit the requirements of the Literacy Framework. It offers real books for beginner readers by top authors and illustrators. There are 27 Leapfrog Rhyme Time stories to choose from:

* hardback